By Pamela Jo Barnaby

Dedicated to Military Children all over the world ...

Chapter 1

A Home for Tenny

Hi, I'm Tenny, short for Tennessee Walker. I'm a tree walker coonhound and this is the story of my big adventure. I live in Pensacola, Florida with my family, or at least I used to. But before we get to that part let me tell you how I became a member of the Walker family.

It all started when I was walking down a back-country road. I was hot and thirsty, and my paws hurt from walking so much. I found a nice shady spot to rest when a lady in a big black van came long and scooped me up. I must have gotten lost because I don't remember much before that. The lady in the big black van was very nice. She was a dog catcher. She gave me water and some yummy snacks. I was so relieved. I don't know if you've ever been to Pensacola in the summer, but it is hot! Whew!

The nice lady took me to a building with lots of other dogs. Some were big and some were small. Some kinds of dogs I had never seen before. I had to get shots and take some pills. The shots hurt! I guess I was sick or something. All the people there were nice. They put me in a little room with a comfy bed. It was so fluffy and soft. I had never had a nice bed like that before.

The next morning, when I woke up, I saw there were lots of other dogs in this place too and they were all saying hi to me, so I said hi back. When dogs say hi, we say, "bark bark bark bark." That's dog for, "hey, how y'all doing?" I would have told them my name, but at that time I didn't really have one. I'll get to that part a little later.

Eventually I figured out what this place was. It was an adoption place for dogs. People would come in and walk around and look at all us dogs and then pick the one they liked the most. If you wanted to be picked to go outside, you had to bark loud and wag your tail and jump up and down. So, every time a person would come, I barked the loudest and I jumped the highest and I wagged my tail, but no one ever picked me to go outside.

After a few days I started to get sad. It seemed like every other dog got to go outside, except for me. I didn't even have a window to look out to see what they were doing. I felt like giving up and just moping around all day on my bed, but then one day a little girl and her mama came walking through looking at all of us dogs. I could tell right away that they were really nice people. Dogs have a way of understanding humans like you wouldn't believe. We know if someone is nice or if we should bite them. These two looked like a great pair and I wanted to go outside with them so bad.

I thought maybe this time I would try a different approach, so I waited and waited until they got right in front of me and I looked up at them and we locked eyes, and I let out my best, "hoooowwwwwwwwllllllll." That's "I'm a hound dog", in dog language. The mama's face lit up with excitement and the little girl laughed so hard.

Well, you know what happened next? I finally got to go outside! The little girl led me out on something called a leash to a small yard outside of the building. I had never been on a leash before. I didn't really know what it was or how to run around and play with her holding me like that, but I didn't let that stop me. I ran to the yard and I jumped, and I played, and I wagged my tail, and the little girl played with me. We had so much fun! Then mama joined in and we all ran around in the yard and played together. It was great!

After a few minutes of running around I was tired. I was thinking they were going to take me back when the dog catcher lady came to talk to mama and the little girl. I just stood quietly and tried to understand what they were saying, dogs can understand humans pretty well. We are very sharp animals. Occasionally, mama would look at me and smile so I would smile back. Dogs can actually smile; it just doesn't look the same as when humans do it. The little girl was tugging on her mama and begging for something. I think she was hungry. The next thing I know, the little girl picked me up into her arms and danced around with me and hugged me so tight. That is when I knew I was going home with them forever.

Chapter 2

Welcome to the Family

The little girl led me out of the yard by the leash again, which I still did not quite get. I tried to chew the leash off my neck, but the dog catcher lady said something that sounded like, "no, bad dog." I didn't know what a no bad dog was at the time, but I was about to find out.

After that we didn't go back into the room with all the other doggies, instead we went into another long narrow room that had a big door. There were pictures on the walls of people holding dogs. The people must have liked the dogs because they all looked so happy. I barked at every picture to say hi but none of the dogs barked back. That's odd I thought, do dogs in pictures not speak?

I waited in this big open area that looked like a playroom with the little girl. The room had all kinds of fun chew toys! I chewed on a yellow squishy ball and then I found a toy that made squeaky sounds! I chewed so much on that squeaky toy that I found the squeaker inside. Right as I was about to investigate this squeaker mom came in and took the little girl by the hand and guess what? I got adopted!

Have you ever ridden in a truck before? Well I have and it's the most fun ever! After we left the building I got to sit in the back seat of a truck with the little girl. She had to sit in a special seat, I guess so she couldn't hang her head out of the window, although I don't know why because that was so much fun. I got to see so much cool stuff on the truck ride. There were so many cars, trucks, and people out and about in Pensacola. Then I heard a super loud noise come from above the truck. I ducked down into the seat and covered my eyes. That was scary! Mom saw me duck and cover and she said not to worry because that noise was the Blue Angels.

I guess these Blue Angels are famous in Pensacola, and they fly all over the city making all kinds of scary loud noises. Eventually I got the courage to get back up from the seat and stick my face out in the wind, but I kept my eyes out for those angels.

Tenny on his way home from the animal shelter. First car ride.

We eventually came to a stop and mama said, "we're home." Mama came and took the little girl out of her seat and I jumped out of the truck too. The little girl walked me into the home, and I looked around. I heard mama saying something to the girl and she kept calling the girl Holly. I think that was her name, Holly.

Holly was small like me and had big blue eyes and puffy cheeks. I licked her face because she smelt like a sugar cookie and she was all sticky. Holly came up to me with a bowl of fresh water and some food. It was little square white blocks in the bowl. I ate them all and they were so tasty. Mama came in the room and said to Holly not to give Tenny marshmallows. "Oh marshmallows",

I thought, that's what I had just eaten. They were so yummy. My mouth as all sticky afterwards, they must be Holly's favorite.

Mama brought me some different food and it was much better. I ate everything because I was so hungry. Holly rubbed my head while I was eating and then she pointed to herself and said "Holly." Yep I think that's her name! I wonder if I have a name. Then Holly pointed to me and said "Tenny." She did this a few times first pointing to herself and saying "Holly", and then pointing to me and repeating "Tenny." That's how I learned my name, Tenny, short for Tennessee. I was the newest member of the Walker family of Pensacola, FL.

Holly and I were best friends right from the start. She always liked to pick me up and squeeze me, sometimes too tight, but I didn't mind because being all alone in that place before wasn't no fun at all. I love being hugged and having someone to play with. And guess what, I had a brother too! His name is Oreo, but he is not that friendly. Mama said he was an old man in cat years. I had never seen a cat before. He was small and his fur was so soft. He does not like to be touched though, and he is not that playful or nice either, matter of fact he can be borderline scary. He was black and white and made all sorts of funny sounds. Cats have such a weird language. I couldn't understand anything he was saying. Hopefully, we will become friends.

When mama opened the back door to the house I bolted out. I never had my very own yard before but now I did. I could run around and play, dig holes, roll in the grass, and bury my bones now in my own space. I liked having a yard to play in, and a mama, and a Holly.

Chapter 3

Big Brother Noah

Later that afternoon the front door flung wide open and another little person ran inside straight at me with eyes wide open and a big smile. And guess what, I had another brother! This one was a little boy and he grabbed me up and squeezed me so tight. Wow, this family likes to give hugs! I heard mama say that his name was Noah and he was at football practice earlier when I first came home. I wonder what football is. I can understand humans for the most part, but some of their words are rather tricky.

Noah is so much fun to play with. He likes to roll around in the dirt like me. We played for a long time that afternoon until mama came outside and said that Noah needed a bath and so do I. What is a bath? That's another one of those silly human words. Mama and Noah started to fill a tub with water and put soap and chew toys inside the tub. I thought that looked like fun, so I grabbed the chew toys and ran. Noah chased me down and tried to get the toy from me. Noah runs fast! Mama came and picked me up and put me in the bathtub. Wow! This is what a bath is! You get to play in the water with your chew toys, and bite the bubbles, and your family splashes around in the water with you. I love baths!

After my bath I smelled so clean and fresh. Mama said no more playing outside today, so we went inside to play. Noah brought me upstairs to see his room. He had a neat room with tons of small toys everywhere. I quickly grabbed one and tried to chew it, but I spit it out. Blah! That was not a chew toy! Mama came in and told Noah to pick up his blocks. That's what I tried to chew, a block? Nope, those are not fun at all.

Holly's room was right across the hall and she had all kinds of fluffy stuffed animal toys. I wondered what it tastes like. So, I grabbed a stuffed turtle and off I ran. Holly tried to chase me down, but she wasn't fast enough. I ran down the hall to the bathroom and then Noah tried to catch me, and I darted right past him, but mama blocked my way and grabbed the turtle. Mama said those same words again the dog catcher lady said, "no bad dog." I think that meant I did something wrong. I remember the dog catcher lady saying those words to me too when I tried to chew the leash. This is kind of how dogs learn. We hear human words repeatedly and eventually it just clicks in our mind. I never bothered that little turtle again. The next time I tried the stuffed pink unicorn, but that didn't go so well either.

After all that excitement I was so tired. Mama was in the kitchen and she was making something that smelled so yummy. I lay down at her feet and watched her cooking. She was tall and had brown hair and brown eyes. She always gave me a smile when she looked at me. I really liked her, and I hoped she will be my mama forever. I was so happy to be in the Walker home. Even though everything was all new to me, I figured I would learn how to be in a family as I go. I had a lot of questions rolling around in my mind. What is football? Why can't I chew the cute little stuffed turtle? What is mama making that smells so delicious?

I didn't remember having a family before. My memory is foggy, but I think I may have gotten lost and my nose took me on a route that didn't lead me back to where I came from. You know sometimes you smell something new and you must go investigate. Dogs have a great sense of smell, but sometimes if you wonder off to far you can get confused. But anyways, I was so happy to finally be home. Maybe my nose led me to the Walker family. My eyes were starting to get heavy after a long day. I slowly drifted off to sleep and dreamed

about that delicious smell that was coming
from mama's oven.

Chapter 4

The Leader of the Pack

Now, this next part of the story is my favorite. When I woke up from my nap there were some big black boots in front of my face. I slowly looked up and attached to those boots was a tall man in a green spotty outfit. He had his hands on his hips and he was looking down at me while I was looking up at him. I gave him a big smile and a few happy barks and then he turned away and talked to mama. I got up and sniffed his butt like any polite dog would do, you know humans don't understand our very delicate communication system. The tall man moved my nose away and walked into the other room, so I followed him. I could instantly tell that he was the person in charge here. Have I mentioned before that dogs are very smart animals? We can sense things and I could tell he was the alpha of the pack, that's dog lingo for "the leader."

He sat down to take off his shiny boots and I went over to assist him. I had a feeling that I needed to show the alpha that I was a helpful new member of the pack. He had so many laces on his boots and they were so shiny it was so hard to resist. I quickly grabbed one and ran upstairs. I wanted to chew those shiny little pieces right off right away. I darted into moms room and jumped up on her big bed and started to chew, but then the alpha came running after me so off I went again. I juked past him and ran into Holly's room and slid under her bed still holding onto the boot. Alpha chased after me again and reached under the bed and grabbed the boot from me. I don't think he appreciated my little game or the chew marks on his boot.

A little later that evening mama put a delicious-smelling dinner on the table for everyone to eat. Now you know dogs have the best noses of any animal, or at least that's what I've always been told. We can track a scent for miles and miles. Mama's food smelled so good that I couldn't resist. After everyone sat down together at the table, I climbed up the stairs and jumped down from the landing onto the table and grabbed a piece of steak. Everyone jumped up and made a big raucous! I instantly turned on my speedy mode and darted into the kitchen. I tried to quickly chew the meat which tasted so good, but just as I was inhaling the food mom came around one corner and the alpha came around the other and guess what? He wanted to play tug of war! He grabbed my steak and started tugging so I tugged back even harder. I love tug of war; it's my favorite game. I tugged and tugged and then I let go, and the alpha fell on his bottom with the steak in his hand.

Then I shouted, "I win," which in dog language is, "bark bark bark bark."

Later that night we were all starting to get a little tired after a terribly busy day, so everyone headed upstairs for bed. I naturally followed Holly up, but the alpha said, "no Tenny, your bed is right here." Then he pointed to a crate in the corner of the living room with a blanket inside. I heard Noah and Holly pleading with him to let me come upstairs. They were both calling him dad, so I think that's his name. Dad wasn't having none of it, I think he was mad about me winning that tug of war game earlier. He opened the door to the crate in the corner and looked at me and said, "go to bed Tenny." I didn't want to sleep downstairs all alone, but I dragged myself into the crate and he shut the door behind me. I slumped down onto the bed inside the crate and started to whine.

The lights were off, and it was dark, and I sure was lonely. I hate being all alone. It reminded me of that place I used to be when they turned the lights off at night, but at least there I had other dogs to talk to. A little bit later I heard something squeaky coming down the stairs. It sounded like it was coming closer to me. I covered my eyes with my front paws but then I heard a voice, it was Holly! Yay I'm saved! Holly opened the door to my crate and we both quietly tip toed upstairs. We snuggled into her big fluffy pink bed and off to sleep I went. I just love Holly. She's my best friend.

Chapter 5

Beach Day

The next morning when I woke up mommy was standing over us with her arms crossed. She said, "that girl, I swear". I don't think I was supposed to be in Holly's bed. Mommy let me outside to potty and then we went to the kitchen together. Mommy is the best cook. She gave me little pieces of sausage and it was so yummy. Mommy said that today they were taking me to the beach. I get so excited to go places and see new things. I love exploring, hmmm I wonder if that's how I got lost in the first place. You know it's so fun to try new things and you never know what awesomeness life may have in store for you. I am so glad I ended up with the Walker family because they love to explore too.

Later that afternoon mama packed a bag of toys and some lunch and we all went in the truck together to the beach. I didn't know exactly what a beach was at first, but it turned out to be so much fun! I ran around and dug big holes in the sand with Holly and I jumped in the water and tried to swim with Noah. I got all sandy and dirty, but it was a blast! I saw some colorful fish swimming around my paws. I tried to bite them, but they all swam away. There were also these crawly things that Noah called crabs on the sand and they would run sideways and try to chase me if I got to close. Mama was watching all of us play and she set up a picnic lunch on the shore for us. Mama is so thoughtful and loving. She brought some of the yummiest treats. She said she made them herself with love. It was the best day ever! We've had lots and lots of beach days since then as a family. Living in Pensacola was great! The sand is so soft and white, and the water is so clear.

Tennys first trip to the beach.

Chapter 6

A Trusty Sidekick

When we got home that afternoon, I was so tired. I plopped down on the couch and took a nice long nap; I think we all did. When I woke up daddy was home. This time he was wearing a tan colored shiny uniform and a big round hat. He had all kinds of colored ribbons and brass things on his chest and his shoes were shiny too. It turns out my dad was a US Navy Chief! Mama, Noah, and Holly seem to be so proud of him. I heard them talking about daddy and how important his job was. Mama said he has a lot of people at work who depend on him. She also said he is a hero and keeps our country safe. I am so proud of my dad.

My proud military family

It took a few tries but eventually dad warmed up to the idea of having a dog and now we are inseparable; I even sleep in the big bed at night snuggled with daddy. He is the best daddy ever! He taught me all kinds of fun tricks. I can sit, stay, bark, give high fives, and give kisses. Daddy also taught me how to catch a fish. Remember when I said we go to the beach a lot? Well, that's an understatement. We go to the beach just about every day. Dad is an expert fisherman and I'm his trusty sidekick. I can swim out in the water, dive under, grab a fish, and bring him back to shore for daddy. I don't think daddy was such a good fisherman before I came along. I like to think I am his lucky charm. Fish are so smelly and slimy. I don't know why daddy likes to catch them.

Where we live on base in Pensacola there are always people walking and biking with their families and daddy always lets me say hello. Sometimes I even do my tricks for folks just to show off. Daddy brings me to the USO when he volunteers, and all the sailors and marines there love to pet me and give me lots of hugs. They miss their own dogs back home, so they give me all their love.

Daddy and I like to run together too, well both mama and daddy like to run, but mom is rather slow, so I usually run fast with daddy. We always wait for mama at the finish line though. Yep, I'm one lucky dog. Life with the Walker bunch is great. We are always out together as a family hiking, fishing, and camping.

Chapter 7

Best Camping Trip Ever

One of my favorite camping trips of all time was when we went to Tennessee. Mama loves the Great Smoky Mountains and the beautiful winding Tennessee River, that is how I got my name, Tenny (short for Tennessee). I remember it was a super long drive and I was getting so cramped up stuffed in the back seat with Noah and Holly, but it was all worth it when we finally stopped.

We had the best camping spot right on the river. I could see why mama and daddy liked it there so much. There were big mountains and lots of wide-open land and fresh air. I loved it! Daddy pitched the tent and set up camp. We played games at the campsite and roasted marshmallows over the fire. You know mama and daddy let me have one because I get to try everything, that's how we learned I was allergic to crab and shrimp, but that's another story.

My favorite part about the Tennessee trip was going on the river in the canoe. I was a bit scared at first because that little boat was really wobbling. If you go too far over to one side you will fall in for sure, so you have to sit just right to balance yourself. After a few falls in the river daddy and I finally figured it out. I had fun though falling in the water. Sometimes I would see a shiny fish, and I would just jump out of the canoe and the whole thing would flip over with daddy inside. I don't think daddy liked it when I did that. Our canoe started to smell like poop because of all the mud so I tried to climb in mama's canoe, but she said no. That was the best trip ever!

Tenny enjoying his canoe ride down the river

Do you know what raccoons are? Well I do now! They are little fat creatures that look like they are wearing glasses. They have human-like hands and like to come out at night and rummage through your stuff. Mama left my dog food out one night on our camping trip and they ate it all! Mama said I should have barked to run them off, but they looked scary, so I just pretended to be asleep. They would come out every night and when we woke in the morning our camp would be a mess. I would lay awake at night and listen to them talking and they sounded similar to Oreo. I wonder if Oreo is part raccoon, he's black and white like them?

Chapter 8

Good Times

Let's get back to the story about the shrimp and the crabs really quick. So, one time we were crabbing, and daddy caught a bunch of crabs in his trap and when he pulled the trap to the shore, one of the crabs wiggled his way out over to me. I was trying to be dad's trusty sidekick like always, so I went over and pushed the crab around a bit with my snout to get him back to dad when suddenly, he pinched me! It hurt so bad! I shook my whole head back and forth again and again, but he wouldn't come off. Dad had to take him off with fishing gloves because that little fella had quite ahold of me. I'll never do that again. That wasn't fun at all.

Dad tried to make me feel better, so he gave me some shrimp. It was so tasty, like I said I pretty much will eat anything. Later that night my throat and my head hurt so bad. I couldn't sleep at all. The next morning my whole throat was swollen, and mama had to take me to the vet. Turns out I'm allergic to both crab and shrimp. Not my fondest memory, but hey at least now I know.

One time I got to be up close and personal with a dolphin. They are super cool animals and they are sort of like dogs, but they live in the water. We were fishing from our boat one day when a happy little dolphin popped his head up right in front of our bow.

I could have sworn he said "hello", but I don't speak dolphin. He swam around right in front of us and splashed his tail. I wanted to jump in the water with him, and I tried to, but daddy caught me first. He said that would probably be a bad idea. The squeaky little dolphin followed our boat around for a bit and then waved by as he swam away. That was a fun day.

Another fun thing I love to do is go to the dog park. Mama takes me to the best park every week so I can see all my friends. There's lots of room to run around and even a pond to splash around in. The best part is I get all muddy and mama has to wash me down with the water hose. Florida is so hot so that cold water sure feels good. I am usually so tired afterwards I sleep all the way home. Sometimes I pretend to be asleep when we get home and mama carries me in the house.

Chapter 9

Ready or Not, Here We Go!

So that was my story before my super big adventure began. You might think that all of the fun stuff we did before this point was the big adventure, but I'm about to tell you an even bigger story.

Things had started to feel a little different in the Walker home. Mama was on her phone and at her desk a lot more and not playing with me as much. I also noticed she also seemed sad sometimes but then excited in the next few minutes. Dogs are smart, we can sense when somethings wrong or when a big change is about to happen. We hadn't been going on any big adventures lately either or exploring new parts of Pensacola like we always did before. Daddy had been home a lot more also which was different because he usually worked during the day. Noah and Holly had been going through their toy boxes and giving away things they didn't play with anymore, and the big thing that really started to worry me was when daddy put all of his fishing gear away.

One day some strange men came to our house and mama made me stay in the back yard all day. I kept looking through the windows and I saw them taking our stuff! They were putting everything into big brown boxes and loading it onto a big truck. It was the most gigantic truck I had ever seen! Noah and Holly seemed to be excited. They came outside to play with me in the back yard and we chased each other around in circles until I was dizzy. They both kept saying something to me that sounded like the word "pan." I wondered what pan means. I had never heard them use that word before.

The next day daddy brought my old crate out from the storage building, you know the one I hated sleeping in when I was a puppy. Yep, it was back in our living room, which was now completely empty, except for the crate. And he also got a smaller one for Oreo! All I kept thinking was "what the heck was going on here." Everyone was in the living room huddled together in a group hug and mama was crying. That made me feel sad to see mama crying. Noah and Holly were so excited for some reason and then Noah came over to me and said, "Tenny, are you ready to move to Japan?" WHAT?

Chapter 10

Military Life

We're moving to Japan! When did that happen? How was I going to get there? Where in the world is Japan? Why do we have to move? All these thoughts were running around in my head. I know we go on lots of new adventures but this one seemed a bit scarier. Now I understood why mama had been so upset earlier and why everything had to be moved out of our house. I heard daddy telling Noah and Holly they were going on a big airplane. What's an airplane? You know dogs can understand a lot of human words, but I had never heard that word airplane before.

The next morning, I was exhausted after all that thinking and worrying. I just wanted to snuggle with daddy and sleep in late, but daddy woke up and said today was the big day. I usually go outside first thing in the morning to sniff around the yard and mark my spots for the day. When I came back in my family was standing all around me in a battle stance position. They had their hands up and their feet apart like they wanted to play, but I had a feeling that wasn't the case. There was a new fluffy dog bed inside my crate, the door was wide open, and Oreo was already inside of his much smaller crate.

"Oh no you don't", I thought to myself. I knew what they were thinking, they wanted me to get inside that crate. Not going to happen. I darted right past Holly, as she tried to grab me, and up the stairs I went.

All the door's upstairs were shut so I was cornered. I turned around and saw daddy coming up the stairs behind me. He lunged to grab me, but I'm faster than lightning so I juked past dad and down the stairs I flew. I scrambled to the kitchen and mama tried to block me, but I zoomed right past her. I ran into the living room knocking Noah over, "sorry Noah", I barked. I was on a mission to escape the crate. Oreo was meowing some gibberish from inside his crate. I imagined he was cheering me on, but you never know with his deceitful self.

Then daddy came downstairs with a glaring look in his eyes and he pointed to the crate and said, "GO." So, I whined a bit but there was no fighting it. There was nowhere to hide and nowhere else to run so I reluctantly hung my head and went inside the crate. Did I mention how I hate being in this box. I don't know what it is about it, but it just doesn't give me a warm and fuzzy feeling.

I didn't know what to think next when daddy shut the door behind me and loaded the crate unto a small cart. Daddy wheeled my crate outside the front door into a van that was waiting in our parking spot. Everyone else loaded into the van too. Daddy sat in the front seat beside the driver and mommy and Holly were in the back seat. Noah sat beside my crate in the middle part of the van. He put his arm on the top of the crate and was patting it like he was trying to reassure me. He peeped through the little holes in the sides and looked in at me. I must've looked afraid in there shaking and whimpering. He poked his little fingers through the front door of the crate and said, "don't be scared Tenny."

I remembered mama talking about how they moved from Virginia to Florida because of daddy's job and it was very scary at first, but then everything was ok. If my family hadn't moved to Florida, they would have never found me. Maybe this move won't be so bad. Maybe we will find lots of new places to explore and new things to tr

I tried to pretend to be happy and smile back at Noah. I remembered mama saying how strong and brave military children are because they move around a lot starting their lives over. They have to be brave and make new friends and start new schools all the time. I wanted to show my

family I was brave too like a military child.
So I took a deep breathe and did my best to
look like I wasn't terrified.

Chapter 11

Tenny's Biggest Adventure Yet

After the long ride in the van we came to the biggest building I had ever seen before. The building had lots of people inside and lots of boxes. I figured maybe that was our stuff that had been boxed up from our house. A man wearing a blue jumpsuit came over and started putting stickers all over my crate. That made it really hard to see out of. I think Oreo's crate was on top of mine because I could hear him making funny cat sounds. Oreo was probably just as confused as I was. The man in the blue jumpsuit talked to mama and daddy for a while and then daddy peered inside my crate door and said he would see me soon. "Bark, bark, bark, bark, bark," that means "get me out of here", in dog language. Mama and daddy waved bye to me through the crate door and I thought, "oh no, they left me." I sure hope they come back. What am I going to do now?

Next, some people picked up my crate and put it on a table, or what I thought was a table, but then it started to move so I'm not sure. It was like my crate was floating through the building on a black winding river. I peered out through the holes in the crate and tried to see if I recognized anything. Nope, nothing, nothing looked familiar to me as I moved through the building. Then I saw the coolest thing ever! It was a huge bird! He or she was white and had large wings with some red writing on the sides. I wasn't sure what kind of bird that was at the time. In Pensacola we had grey herons that would come up to us while daddy and I were fishing. We named one bird Leroy and I always tried to chase him off when he got to close, but I don't think I could chase this big bird away.

I barked to say hello to the big bird, but no reply. Maybe the bird was sleeping. Then the weirdest thing ever happened. The back part of the bird, where the poop comes out, opened! Yes, and the blue suited men wheeled my crate right inside. I was starting to think this wasn't a bird at all. Maybe this is the airplane daddy was talking about this morning.

So, there I was being wheeled up a ramp inside of an airplane, or a sleeping bird butt, which ever one it was. There were a lot of crates inside with dogs and cats. It reminded me of the place I was before I found my family. It was cold and scary, and I didn't see mom or dad or Noah or Holly anywhere. The only comforting thought was knowing that Oreo was above me in his crate too, oh wait, he's gone! Someone took Oreo! I started to bark to alert everyone that my mean cat brother Oreo was missing, but people just came over to the door of my crate and called me, "good boy", and said "what a cutie." I barked so much that my throat hurt.

After a while longer I felt some movement. It seemed like the whole room was shaking and it was loud. The loud noise reminded me of being home watching the Blue Angels fly by with daddy. What in the world was happening? Was I going to Japan now?

Chapter 12

Hello Sugar!

Hours and hours slowly dragged by and occasionally, someone would come and check on me. I'd bark to say hello and they would tell me that we're almost there. Mama had attached a plastic bottle to my crate so I could have water. It took me a while, but I figured this water bottle thing out. You had to roll the ball inside the straw with your tongue. It felt funny but I liked it, and I was so thirsty after all that barking. Mama also put my special blanket inside the crate so that was comforting too. I missed mama so much. I wished she was there to comfort me. She always lets me lay my head on her lap and she pets me until I fell asleep.

I was so bored inside my crate, there was nothing to do. I heard a noise coming from the back side of my crate. It sounded like another dog. I turned around and peeped out of the little holes in the back wall and there was another crate backed up against mine. Inside was a fluffy white dog. She said, "bark bark bark bark bark", which means, "hi, my name is Sugar." I thought to myself, "oh what a tasty name, I love sugar!" Mom would always give me sugary sweets. I know dogs are not supposed to have cookies and brownies and things, but like I said my mom is the best, and I do eat anything.

Sugar said that she was moving to Japan too. It was nice to meet a new friend. We talked for the rest of the plane ride. Sugar said that she has flown on planes lots of times and it wasn't so bad. She told me what would happen when we landed and assured me that I would see my family again soon. Sugar made the rest of the plane ride so much more bearable.

I hoped Oreo was doing ok. Hopefully, he had found a new friend. I wondered what cats talk about. You just never know. Oreo and I had never really had a real conversation since I couldn't understand him. Plus, he always looked so annoyed with me. One time I was laying on mama's lap and Oreo came over and startled me, so I jumped up. I must have scared him because he swatted my nose and made it bleed. His cute little cat paws move so quickly, I didn't see it coming. He's like a cute little fluffy ninja.

After a while it felt like the plane was starting to shake. All the people who were walking by to check on me were now strapped into their seats. We must be landing, I thought to myself. Sugar had told me what to expect so I was ready to get out of this crate and stretch my legs. Then the plane made a big sound and I fell over inside my crate. "Boy that was a doozy", I barked. I checked on Sugar and she was ok. She said, "we just landed." Yay! I was so excited to finally be in Japan.

I heard a loud voice come over a speaker that was saying something in human language. Only thing I could pick out was the word Japan. I was so happy to not be flying anymore and to be getting out of this box soon. Sugar said usually the people will come and get us shortly after we land. I was so happy that I met Sugar. I told her "thank you for being my new friend", which in dog is, "bark bark bark".

Chapter 13

Konnichiwa Tennessee Walker

A while later a group of men came to load our crates. A short man in a black suit came to my crate door and said, "konnichiwa!" I had never heard that word before, so I barked back, "bark bark bark bark", which meant "get me out of here", in dog. The man loaded my crate onto a large cart. Next, I was wheeled down the ramp outside of the plane and into a building. There I was still sitting in my crate when suddenly, my family was there! I was so excited to see them again.

I let out my best coonhound, "howwwwwwllllll". I was jumping with joy inside the crate. I really wanted to get out of there. Mama and daddy talked to the lady in charge and off we went. Daddy loaded my crate onto another cart and wheeled me outside. It was so nice to see and feel the sunshine again. Daddy opened my crate the moment we got outside and I jumped up and gave him the biggest hug and licked his face. I hugged mama and Noah and Holly too. Group hug! It was so nice to be together again, and guess who also made it to Japan, Oreo! Yep Oreo was here too. We were all together again. I was so happy to see their faces, even my mean cat brother.

The long plane ride brought us to our new home in Yokosuka, Japan. It turned out daddy has a new job here onboard a big ship called the USS Ronald Reagan. Japan is going to be a lot different and take some time to get used to, but I'm excited for the new adventures we will have together. Wherever we are together that's where home is. I just know this will be a great new start for the Walker family.

Holly, Tenny, and Noah in Yokosuka, Japan.

(USS Ronald Reagan in the background)

Pamela Barnaby is a navy spouse of seventeen years and mother of two. She currently resides in Yokosuka, Japan with her family. Her husband, David Barnaby, is stationed on USS Ronald Reagan, where Pam also serves as a command ombudsman. Pam is a passionate volunteer on base with many organizations including: the USO, Chief Spouse Association, and the base chapel. She also works as a substitute teacher for Dodea schools. In her free time, she enjoys writing, exercising, photography, traveling, and exploring with her family.

Noah, Tenny, and Holly are still the best of friends.

Oreo is still a grouchy old man, in cat years.

Made in the USA
Monee, IL
15 December 2022